SHADOWS OF FEAR

A PSYCHOLOGICAL THRILLER

PUSKAR DEBNATH

Made with ♥ on the Notion Press Platform
www.notionpress.com

To the countless women and men who have suffered from the trauma of stalking and harassment. May this book shed light on the darkness that plagues our society and empowers all those who have been victimized. You are not alone, and your experiences are valid. May this story be a source of hope and healing for all those who have faced the shadows of fear.

To the advocates, law enforcement officers, and organizations who work tirelessly to support survivors and combat stalking and harassment. Your dedication and commitment to this cause is a beacon of hope for all those who have been impacted by this crime. Thank you for your tireless efforts to make our communities safer and more just.

To my loved ones who have supported me throughout the writing of this book. Your encouragement, patience, and love have meant the world to me. Without you, this book would not have been possible. Thank you for being my guiding light through the shadows of fear.

Contents

Foreword

In "Shadows of Fear," we are taken on a journey into the terrifying world of stalking and harassment. This book sheds light on the devastating impact these crimes can have on individuals and communities, and the importance of taking action to prevent and address them.

Through the eyes of our protagonist, Jennifer, we witness the insidious nature of stalking and the trauma it inflicts upon its victims. We see the psychological toll it takes, the constant fear and anxiety that lingers, and the ways it can tear apart one's sense of safety and control.

But amidst the darkness, there is hope. Jennifer's bravery and resilience remind us that there is a way out of the shadows of fear. With the support of loved ones, the guidance of professionals, and the strength of one's own will, it is possible to survive and overcome this trauma.

"Shadows of Fear" is a powerful and timely reminder of the importance of acknowledging and addressing the issue of stalking and harassment in our communities. It is a call to action for all of us to stand up against these crimes and support those who have been impacted by them.

I am honored to introduce this book and invite you to join me in taking a stand against stalking and harassment. Together, we can create a safer and more just world for all.

Foreword

Preface

This book is a work of fiction, but it is rooted in the reality of the trauma and fear that stalking and harassment can cause. As an author, I felt compelled to shine a light on this issue and explore the experiences of those who have been impacted by it.

While the story and characters are fictional, I have drawn inspiration from real-life stories of stalking and harassment survivors. I have also consulted with professionals in the fields of psychology and law enforcement to ensure that the portrayal of these crimes is accurate and sensitive.

It is my hope that "Shadows of Fear" will not only entertain readers but also raise awareness about the devastating impact of stalking and harassment. I believe that by bringing these issues to light, we can start to break down the stigma and shame that often surrounds them.

I also hope that this book serves as a source of validation and support for those who have experienced stalking and harassment. You are not alone, and your experiences are valid. May this story remind you that you deserve to be heard, believed, and supported.

Thank you for embarking on this journey with me. I hope that "Shadows of Fear" leaves you with a deeper understanding of the impact of stalking and harassment and a renewed commitment to creating a safer and more just world.

Preface

Acknowledgements

I would like to express my heartfelt gratitude to everyone who has supported me in the creation of this book.

First and foremost, I would like to thank the survivors of stalking and harassment who shared their stories with me. Your bravery and resilience in the face of trauma have inspired me beyond words. I am honored to have been entrusted with your stories and am committed to using this book as a platform to raise awareness about the impact of these crimes.

I would also like to thank the professionals in the fields of psychology and law enforcement who generously shared their expertise and insights with me. Your guidance was invaluable in ensuring the accuracy and sensitivity of the portrayal of stalking and harassment in this book.

To my editor, thank you for your unwavering support, guidance, and encouragement throughout the writing process. Your feedback helped shape this book into what it is today.

To my family and friends, thank you for your love, patience, and understanding. Your unwavering support has been the foundation upon which this book was built.

Finally, to the readers, thank you for embarking on this journey with me. I hope that "Shadows of Fear" leaves you with a deeper understanding of the impact of stalking and harassment and a renewed commitment to creating a safer and more just world.

Prologue

Jennifer had always felt safe walking to the library. It was only a few blocks away from her apartment, and the route was well-lit and populated. But on this particular day, she couldn't shake the feeling that someone was following her.

She turned around, but saw no one. Still, the sense of unease persisted. As she walked faster, she heard footsteps behind her. She turned again, but the person behind her quickly ducked behind a building. Jennifer's heart raced as she quickened her pace, now certain that she was being followed.

This was the beginning of a nightmare that would haunt Jennifer for months to come. A stalker had fixated on her, leaving threatening messages and following her everywhere she went. She lived in constant fear, wondering if she would ever be able to reclaim her sense of safety and security.

"Shadows of Fear" tells Jennifer's story, exploring the insidious nature of stalking and the trauma it inflicts upon its victims. It is a story of courage, resilience, and hope, reminding us that even in the darkest of moments, there is a way out of the shadows of fear.

CHAPTER ONE

THE BEGGINING

In the small town of Millfield, Jennifer's life was an ordinary one. She had a job as a librarian and lived alone in her small apartment. But something had been bothering her for a few days. A feeling that she was being watched, followed, but she couldn't quite put her finger on it.

She woke up feeling strange and anxious, the feeling of being watched still present. She looked out of her window, trying to find anything out of the ordinary, but nothing seemed to be amiss. The streets were empty, and the sun was just beginning to rise. Nevertheless, Jennifer couldn't shake off the feeling that something was wrong.

As she made her way to work, Jennifer heard footsteps behind her. She turned around, but no one was there. Her heart started racing as she began to walk faster, but the footsteps grew faster too. The feeling of being followed was still there, and she couldn't shake it off.

Jennifer reached the library and quickly locked the door behind her. She turned around, and there was no one there. She thought she was losing her mind, but the feeling of being watched lingered.

CHAPTER TWO

THE VISITOR

Jennifer couldn't shake the feeling of being watched and followed, and it only grew worse as the days went by. She had become hyper-aware of her surroundings, constantly looking over her shoulder and jumping at every sound. Her colleagues noticed her strange behavior, and she tried to brush it off as just being stressed from work.

One day, as Jennifer was closing up the library, she saw a man standing across the street, watching her. He was tall, dressed in all black, and wore a cap that covered most of his face. Jennifer's heart started racing, and she quickly locked the door and rushed back to her apartment.

She knew she had to do something about it, so she decided to install security cameras around her apartment. She also started to carry pepper spray with her everywhere she went.

Days passed, and Jennifer thought she had finally managed to get a grip on her paranoia. But one night, she heard a knock at her door. She peered through the peephole and saw the same man from the library. Her heart started racing, and she quickly grabbed her pepper spray.

"Who are you, and what do you want?" she asked, her voice shaking.

"I'm sorry to bother you, miss. My name is John, and I live in the apartment across from yours. I noticed that you have security cameras installed, and I was wondering if you could help me install some as well. I'm new to the building, and I don't know anyone else who could help me," the man said, his voice smooth and friendly.

Jennifer hesitated for a moment, but then she remembered that she had seen the man watching her from across the street. She decided to take a chance and let him in.

They worked on the security cameras together, and John seemed like a perfectly normal and friendly guy. He told her that he had moved to Millfield for a new job and was still getting used to the area. Jennifer started to relax, and they chatted about their interests and hobbies.

As they finished up, John thanked Jennifer for her help and promised to return the favor someday. He said goodbye, and Jennifer felt relieved that she had finally made a new friend in the building.

But as soon as she closed the door, the feeling of being watched returned. She looked out of the window and saw John walking back to his apartment, but something felt off. She couldn't quite put her finger on it, but there was something about John that didn't sit right with her.

The next few days were uneventful, and Jennifer started to believe that her paranoia had gotten the best of her. But one night, she woke up to find John standing at the foot of her bed. He had a knife in his hand, and his eyes were filled with malice.

Jennifer screamed and tried to run, but John grabbed her by the arm and dragged her back. She kicked and fought, but he was too strong. He pinned her down, and she realized that she was in grave danger.

But just as she thought it was the end, the door to her apartment burst open, and the police stormed in. John was arrested, and Jennifer was taken to the hospital.

The police told her that John was a known criminal who had been targeting women in the area. He had been watching Jennifer for weeks, waiting for the perfect opportunity to strike.

Jennifer couldn't believe it. She had let her guard down, thinking that John was just a friendly neighbor. She had almost lost her life because of her naivety.

From that day on, Jennifer made a vow to never let her guard down again. She knew that there were dangerous people out there, and she had to be prepared for anything. She had learned a valuable lesson about trust and

after the incident, Jennifer struggled with PTSD and anxiety, but she sought help and slowly began to heal. She moved to a new town and started a new job, hoping to leave the memories of her ordeal behind.

But the trauma had left a mark on her, and she became hyper-aware of her surroundings, constantly looking over her shoulder and being cautious of new people. It took a long time, but eventually, Jennifer found some sense of peace and security.

However, the memory of John and what he had almost done to her lingered. She couldn't help but wonder if there were other dangerous people out there, lurking in the shadows, waiting to strike.

The experience had taught her that danger could be hidden behind friendly faces, and she had to be careful of who she let into her life. She had to trust her instincts and always be prepared for the worst.

Jennifer had survived a terrifying ordeal, and it had changed her in ways that she never thought possible. She had learned the hard way that the world could be a dangerous place, but she had also learned that she had the strength to overcome it.

CHAPTER THREE

THE REAPPEARANCE

Years had passed since the incident with John, and Jennifer had moved on with her life. She had worked hard to overcome her fears and had finally found a sense of peace and stability.

But one day, as she was walking to her new job, she saw a familiar figure walking towards her. It was John.

Jennifer froze in fear, unable to move or speak. She had thought that he was in prison, serving a long sentence for his crimes. But there he was, walking towards her with a smile on his face.

"Jennifer, it's so good to see you again," John said, his voice smooth and friendly.

Jennifer couldn't believe it. How had he found her? Why was he out of prison? The questions raced through her mind, and she felt a sense of panic rising within her.

She tried to run, but John caught up to her and grabbed her by the arm. "Don't be afraid, Jennifer. I just want to talk to you," he said, his grip tightening.

Jennifer's heart was racing, and she knew that she was in danger. She tried to pull away, but John was too strong. She screamed for help, hoping that someone would hear her.

Just as she thought it was the end, a group of people came running towards them. They had heard her screams and had come to her rescue.

John fled, and Jennifer was taken to the hospital, shaken and traumatized once again. The police were called, and they launched an investigation to find John.

But as the days passed, Jennifer began to realize that John had not been the one who had found her. Someone else had brought him back into her life, someone who had been watching her all along.

She couldn't shake the feeling of being watched, and she knew that she was not safe. She had to be careful, and she had to find out who was behind the reappearance of John.

Jennifer started to investigate, digging deep into her past and trying to find any clues that could lead her to the truth. She talked to her old colleagues, revisited the places where she had lived before, and tried to remember anything that could be relevant.

And finally, she found something. A letter, sent to her anonymously, with a single message: "I'm watching you."

Jennifer's heart sank as she realized that the danger was not over yet. Someone was still out there, watching her every move, and she had to find out who it was before it was too late.

To be continued...

CHAPTER FOUR

THE HUNT

Jennifer knew that she had to take action. She couldn't just sit and wait for the stalker to make a move. She had to find out who it was and put an end to it once and for all.

She started to investigate more, looking for any clues that could lead her to the stalker's identity. She installed security cameras in her apartment and carried pepper spray with her at all times.

But the stalker was one step ahead of her. Every time she thought she had found a lead, it turned out to be a dead end. She was growing more and more frustrated with each passing day.

One day, Jennifer received a phone call from an unknown number. She hesitated before answering, but curiosity got the better of her.

"Hello?" she said, her voice shaky.

"Hello, Jennifer. You don't know me, but I know you. I've been watching you for a long time now," the voice on the other end of the line said.

Jennifer's heart was racing, and she knew that she was in danger. "Who are you?" she asked, trying to keep her voice steady.

"You'll find out soon enough. But for now, I just want to let you know that I'm watching you, and I know everything about you. You can't hide from me," the voice said before hanging up.

Jennifer was terrified. She had to do something, but she didn't know what. She decided to contact the police and tell them everything.

The police took her seriously and started an investigation. They told her to be careful and advised her to stay with a friend or family member until they found the stalker.

Jennifer packed her bags and went to stay with her sister, hoping that she would be safe there. But she couldn't shake the feeling of being watched, even in her sister's house.

Days turned into weeks, and Jennifer was growing more and more anxious. She felt like she was living in a constant state of fear, never knowing when the stalker would strike.

And then, one day, it happened. Jennifer was walking back to her sister's house from the grocery store when she felt someone grab her from behind. She tried to scream, but a hand covered her mouth.

The stalker had finally made his move.

To be continued...

CHAPTER FIVE

THE CONFRONTATION

Jennifer's heart was racing as the stalker dragged her into an alleyway. She was trying to fight him off, but he was too strong.

"Stop struggling, Jennifer. It's no use. You're mine now," the stalker whispered into her ear.

Jennifer's mind was racing, trying to come up with a plan to get away from the stalker. And then, she remembered the pepper spray she had in her pocket.

With all her might, Jennifer managed to break free from the stalker's grasp and sprayed him with pepper spray. He stumbled back, his eyes burning and coughing.

Jennifer didn't waste a second. She ran as fast as she could, not looking back. She didn't know where she was going, but she had to get away from the stalker.

After what felt like hours, Jennifer finally stopped running. She was in a park, surrounded by trees and greenery. She collapsed on a bench, panting and sweating.

Suddenly, she heard footsteps behind her. She turned around, ready to fight the stalker off again. But it was a police officer.

"Are you okay, miss? We received a call about a woman being attacked in the alleyway," the police officer said.

Jennifer told the officer everything that had happened, and they launched a search for the stalker. But he was nowhere to be found.

Jennifer went back to her sister's house, shaken and traumatized once again. She couldn't believe that the stalker had almost gotten to her. She decided that she had to take matters into her own hands.

She went back to the library, where she had worked before. She started to go through the security footage from the day John had reappeared in her life. And that's when she saw it.

A figure in the background, watching her every move. She zoomed in on the face, and it was someone she knew. Someone she had worked with at the library.

Jennifer's heart sank as she realized that the stalker had been right in front of her all along.

To be continued...

The police launched a search for the stalker, but he was nowhere to be found. Jennifer went back to her sister's house, shaken and traumatized once again. She couldn't believe that the stalker had almost gotten to her. She decided that she had to take matters into her own hands.

She went back to the library, where she had worked before. She started to go through the security footage from the day John had reappeared in her life. And that's when she saw it.

A figure in the background, watching her every move. She zoomed in on the face, and it was someone she knew. Someone she had worked with at the library.

Jennifer's heart sank as she realized that the stalker had been right in front of her all along. She couldn't believe that it was someone she knew and trusted.

She decided to confront the person and went to the library the next day. She tried to act as normal as possible, not wanting to give away that she knew.

But as soon as she saw the person's face, her heart sank. It was John, a colleague at the library.

Jennifer's mind was racing. She didn't know what to do. She had to confront John, but she didn't know how. She couldn't just accuse him without any proof.

So she decided to play along, trying to get more information from him. She pretended that everything was normal and even talked to him about the stalker, trying to see if he would slip up.

And he did. John said something that made Jennifer realize that he was the stalker. She confronted him, and he admitted everything.

John had been obsessed with Jennifer for years, watching her from a distance and gathering information about her. He had even followed her to the new town when she had moved away.

Jennifer couldn't believe that someone she had worked with every day had been stalking her. She felt violated and betrayed.

She reported John to the police, and he was arrested. She couldn't shake the feeling of being watched, even after he was behind bars.

But she knew that she had to move on with her life. She couldn't let the stalker control her anymore.

To be continued...

CHAPTER SIX

THE AFTERMATH

After John's arrest, Jennifer found it hard to trust anyone. She felt like everyone was watching her, waiting for the right moment to attack her.

She started attending therapy sessions, hoping to overcome her trauma. The therapist helped her to understand that she wasn't to blame for what had happened, and that it was normal to feel the way she did.

Jennifer slowly started to rebuild her life. She went back to work at the library, but she couldn't shake the feeling of being watched.

One day, as she was leaving the library, she noticed a man standing on the other side of the street. He was staring at her, and Jennifer felt a familiar sense of fear wash over her.

She didn't know what to do. She had thought that John was the only stalker, but now it seemed like someone else was watching her.

Jennifer started to carry pepper spray with her at all times. She couldn't let herself be vulnerable again.

But as the days passed, Jennifer realized that the man wasn't following her. He was just a passerby who happened to be looking in her direction.

Slowly but surely, Jennifer started to let go of her fear. She started to trust people again, and she felt like she was finally moving on with her life.

However, there was one thing that still bothered her. She had never found out why John had started stalking her in the first place. What had driven him to become so obsessed with her?

She started to do some research, trying to find out more about John's past. And that's when she found something shocking.

John had been in a relationship with a woman who looked strikingly similar to Jennifer. They had broken up years ago, but John had never been able to get over her.

Jennifer realized that she had been a substitute for John's ex-girlfriend. He had been trying to recreate their relationship with her.

She felt sick to her stomach. She had been nothing more than a pawn in John's twisted game.

To be continued...

CHAPTER SEVEN

CLOSURE

Jennifer felt angry and betrayed. She couldn't believe that John had used her like that. But she also felt relieved. She finally knew why he had been stalking her.

She decided that she needed to confront John. She went to visit him in prison, and she asked him why he had done it.

At first, John was hesitant to talk. But eventually, he opened up. He told Jennifer that he had been in love with his ex-girlfriend for years, and he had never been able to let go.

When he saw Jennifer, he saw a chance to recreate his relationship with his ex. He started to stalk her, trying to find out as much as he could about her. He even broke into her apartment and stole some of her belongings, hoping to create a connection between them.

Jennifer was horrified by what she heard. She couldn't believe that someone could be so obsessed with another person.

But as she listened to John, she realized that she had been blaming herself for what had happened. She had thought that she had done something to make John start stalking her. But now she knew that it was all his fault.

Jennifer left the prison feeling a sense of closure. She knew that she could finally move on with her life.

CHAPTER EIGHT

THE NEW BEGINNING

Jennifer decided to leave Millfield and start fresh somewhere else. She had loved the small town, but it had too many bad memories for her.

She packed up her belongings and moved to a bigger city. She found a new job and a new apartment, and she started to rebuild her life.

It wasn't easy, but Jennifer was determined to move forward. She made new friends and started to explore the city. She even started dating again, something she never thought she would be able to do.

Jennifer knew that she would never forget what had happened to her, but she also knew that it was a part of her past. She had survived the stalker, and she was stronger because of it.

Jennifer moved to the city with nothing but a few boxes of belongings and a sense of determination. She was starting over, and she was excited to see what the future held.

The first few weeks in the city were tough. Jennifer felt lonely and out of place. But she knew that she needed to push through the discomfort and make the most of her new life.

She threw herself into her work and quickly made friends with her coworkers. They showed her around the city and introduced her to new people.

One day, Jennifer met a man named Alex at a coffee shop. He was charming and funny, and they hit it off right away. They exchanged numbers and started dating soon after.

Alex was everything Jennifer had been looking for in a partner. He was kind, supportive, and always made her feel like she was the most important person in the world. They spent countless hours exploring the city and trying new things.

Jennifer was happy, but she couldn't shake the feeling that something was off. She would sometimes wake up in the middle of the night, feeling like she was being watched.

At first, she thought it was just her imagination. But as the weeks went by, the feeling grew stronger. She started to notice a man following her on her way home from work.

Jennifer was terrified. She had been through this before, and she didn't want to relive that experience. She confided in Alex, and he immediately offered to help.

Together, they worked out a plan to catch the stalker. They set up a hidden camera outside Jennifer's apartment and waited for the stalker to appear.

Days turned into weeks, but they never caught a glimpse of the stalker. Jennifer started to wonder if she was just imagining things again.

But one day!

to be continued...

CHAPTER NINE

RETURN OF TERROR

one day, as Jennifer was leaving the library, she saw someone she never thought she would see again - John.

She froze as John approached her. He had lost weight and looked much different than she remembered. But the same cold, calculating look was still in his eyes.

"Hello, Jennifer," John said, his voice smooth and confident.

Jennifer tried to walk away, but John grabbed her arm. "I just want to talk," he said.

Jennifer's heart was pounding in her chest. She didn't know what to do. She tried to pull away from John, but he wouldn't let go.

"Please, just leave me alone," Jennifer begged.

But John just smiled. "I'm afraid I can't do that, Jennifer. You see, I've been following you. Watching you. And I've realized something."

"What?" Jennifer asked, her voice shaking.

"I've realized that I can't live without you," John said. "I need you, Jennifer. And I won't let anyone else have you."

Jennifer felt sick to her stomach. She had been down this road before, and she knew how it ended. But this time, she was stronger. She had Alex and her friends to support her.

"Let go of me, John," Jennifer said firmly. "I'm not going to be your victim anymore."

John's smile turned into a scowl. "You think you're so smart, Jennifer. But you'll see. You'll see what I'm capable of."

With that, John let go of Jennifer's arm and walked away. Jennifer stood there, trembling. She knew that she couldn't let John get the better of her. She had to take action.

She called the police and reported John's presence. She also told Alex and her friends what had happened.

They all rallied around her, making sure that she was safe and supported. Jennifer felt stronger than she ever had before.

Days turned into weeks, and Jennifer didn't see or hear from John again. She started to feel like she was finally free of him.

But then, one day, Jennifer received a letter in the mail. It was addressed to her, and she didn't recognize the handwriting.

She opened the letter and read the contents. Her heart sank as she realized that it was from John. He had written about how much he loved her and how he couldn't live without her.

Jennifer felt sick. She didn't know what to do. She couldn't go through this again.

But then, she had an idea. She called the police and asked for their help.

Together, they set up a sting operation to catch John. They lured him to a park, where Jennifer was waiting with the police.

When John arrived, he was arrested on the spot. Jennifer watched as he was taken away, feeling a sense of relief wash over her.

After that day, Jennifer felt like a weight had been lifted from her shoulders. She knew that she was finally free of John and his twisted games.

She and Alex continued to build their life together, and Jennifer felt like she had finally found the happiness and peace that she had been searching for.

The Uncovering Truth: The End

After John's arrest, Jennifer felt like she could finally move on with her life. She continued to work at the library, spending her days surrounded by books and happy customers. Her relationship with Alex continued to blossom, and they made plans for the future together.

But one day, as Jennifer was organizing books in the library, she noticed something strange. A book had been returned, but it didn't have a title or author listed on the cover. Instead, it was covered in plain, brown paper.

Jennifer's curiosity got the best of her, and she opened the book. Inside, she found a series of disturbing messages written in code. They seemed to be directed at her, and they referenced John and their past relationship.

Jennifer's heart started racing. She knew that this had to be connected to John somehow, but she didn't know how.

She took the book to the police, and they began to investigate. They soon discovered that the book had been sent to the library by someone using a fake name and address. They couldn't trace it back to John, but they knew that it had to be connected to him somehow.

Jennifer was scared, but she knew that she had to find out the truth. She began to dig deeper, looking for any clues that might lead her to the person behind the mysterious book.

Her investigation led her to a small, rundown apartment building on the outskirts of town. She knocked on the door of the unit that the book had been mailed from, and was surprised when a young man answered.

He seemed nervous and twitchy, but he invited Jennifer inside. As she looked around the apartment, she realized that it was filled with strange symbols and codes. The young man explained that he was a hacker and that he had been paid to send the book to the library.

Jennifer pressed him for more information, and he eventually admitted that John had hired him to send the book. He didn't know what the messages meant, but he had been paid well for his services.

Jennifer knew that she had to take this information to the police. She also realized that this was just the tip of the iceberg. John was still out there, and he was still obsessed with her.

She and Alex made plans to move away from the city, to a place where John would never be able to find them. They left everything behind and started fresh, hoping that they could finally put the past behind them.

But as they settled into their new home, Jennifer couldn't shake the feeling that something wasn't right. She started to notice strange things happening around the house - objects moved or missing, strange noises in the night.

She tried to convince herself that it was just her imagination, but she couldn't shake the feeling that John was still out there, watching her, waiting for his chance to strike.

One night, as Jennifer and Alex were asleep in their new home, they were awoken by a loud crash. They rushed to investigate and found that their front door had been kicked in.

As they stood there, stunned, John emerged from the darkness. He was more twisted and unhinged than ever before, and he had a dangerous glint in his eye.

Jennifer and Alex knew that they were in danger. They tried to run, but John was faster. He cornered them in the living room, a crazed grin on his face.

But then, something strange happened. A figure emerged from the darkness, wielding a large knife. It was the hacker from the apartment building.

He had followed Jennifer and Alex and had been watching their new home. When he saw John break-in, he knew that he had to act.

He fought John off with the knife, giving Jennifer and Alex enough time to escape. They ran out of the house and called the police, who arrived on the scene within minutes.

When they searched the house, they found John's lifeless body on the floor. The hacker had taken matters into his own hands and had ended John's twisted obsession for good.

Jennifer and Alex were shaken by the events but relieved that they were finally safe. They knew that they would never forget the horrors that they had endured, but they were determined to move forward with their lives.

In the end, they found solace in each other's arms, knowing that they had faced their fears and come out on the other side. They knew that they would always be connected by the dark, twisted past that they had shared, but they were also connected by a deep love that had survived against all odds.

As they looked towards the future, Jennifer and Alex knew that they would always be haunted by the memories of John and his twisted games. But they also knew that they were strong enough to overcome anything, as long as they had each other.

hope u loved the story...

Printed by Libri Plureos GmbH in Hamburg, Germany